AF227690

Jersey Publications
151, Les Quennevais Park,
St. Brelade, Jersey. JE3 8JU
Channel islands

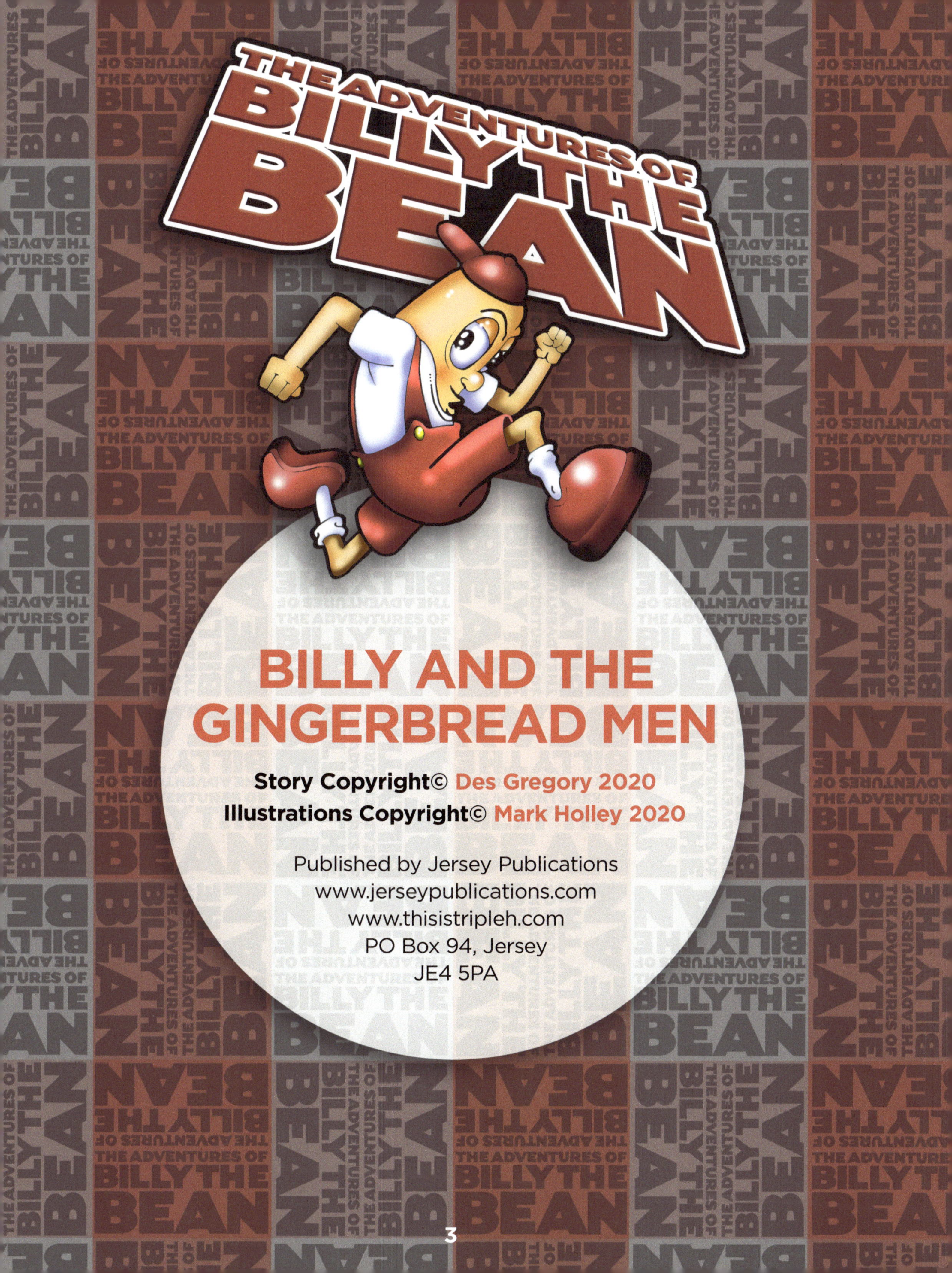

BILLY AND THE GINGERBREAD MEN

Story Copyright© Des Gregory 2020
Illustrations Copyright© Mark Holley 2020

Published by Jersey Publications
www.jerseypublications.com
www.thisistripleh.com
PO Box 94, Jersey
JE4 5PA

SWEET
Home HoMe
4

T he smell of baking bread wafted up the stairs and into the room where Billy Bean was sleeping. As he lay in bed, his nostrils started twitching as the aroma became stronger. Downstairs in the kitchen, his mother was hard at work, with fresh bread already in the oven, and a steak pie ready to follow it into the oven, was on the nearby dresser, awaiting its turn. Meanwhile she turned her attentions to making Billy's favourite, gingerbread men.

Upstairs, the aromas from the kitchen, teased Billy as he lay in bed, while the bread came out of the oven, and the pie went in. Then when the pie came out, and the gingerbread men went in, he could stand it no more. He jumped out of bed, washed and dressed in double quick time, before running down the stairs.

"That took you longer than I thought," his mother smiled as he clattered into the kitchen.

"I just couldn't resist any longer," Billy admitted.

"Right breakfast then, beans I suppose as usual?" Billy nodded eagerly. His mother busied herself warming the beans in a saucepan, and toasting some bread under the grill.

"There we are," she said placing his breakfast in front of him. She cleared a space on the rest of the table. "Right Billy, the gingerbread men are ready, so I'll put them here on the table to cool. You'll make sure you don't touch the trays till they're cold won't you."

"Yes mother I'll be careful," Billy replied as he started his breakfast.

"I'm off to the market now, I won't be long," she said as she left the house.

It wasn't long after his mother had left the house, when Billy thought he saw a movement on the baking tray nearest him. He put the spoon he was using down in his dish, and stared at the baking tray. He reached out touching the tray quickly in case it was very hot, but it was not too hot, and nothing seemed out of place. He continued with his breakfast. Then...there it was again, he saw something out of the corner of his eye. He looked up suddenly at the baking tray, to his amazement, the gingerbread man nearest to him had lifted its head up off the tray. Billy

couldn't believe his eyes; he rubbed his eyes with the back of his hands, and then looked back at the tray. There was no mistake, the gingerbread man was starting to sit up, Billy's mouth dropped open in disbelief, it couldn't be, could it? But it was, there, right in front of him. Then the gingerbread man turned his head towards him.

"Hello," he said. Now Billy couldn't believe his ears.

"H...H...Hello," he spluttered in reply. Then the gingerbread man stood up, getting taller and taller. He stepped off the baking tray on to the table, then jumped down to the floor and kept growing until he was about the same height as Billy. Then he leaned over the table and started prodding the other gingerbread men one by one.

"Come on, come on wake up all of you," he prodded each one, until all twenty four of them were on the floor, and growing until the room was full. Then they all trooped out into the garden.

"Right lads," the one who woke up first seemed to be in charge. "Line up in fours, and we'll march up to the forest."

"Forest? You mean up there in the woods?" Billy said.

"That's right, tonight is the night you know."

"What night?" Billy asked.

"It's the Woodland Ball night, that's what night it is. Every year, on the second Wednesday of August."

"Well I've never heard of it," Billy retorted.

"Well of course you haven't," the gingerbread man replied. "That's because you've not been magic before, have you?"

"But I'm not magic," Billy confessed. He didn't really know whether he was magic or not, but then he thought, perhaps if I can make myself smaller and bigger, talk to animals, and even disappear, I suppose I must be. "Can I come then? To the Ball that is?"

"Come? What do you mean come? Of course you're coming; you're the band's conductor."

"What band?" Billy was confused.

"We're the band," the gingerbread man said. "We're musicians

you know, we play the music for the Ball."

"Well I didn't know that did I," Billy retorted. "So if you're musicians, where are your instruments then?"

"Up there," the gingerbread man pointed to the woods above Secret Valley. "We leave them there all the time, so then they're ready for us when we come back."

"Oh, I see," Billy said not really seeing at all. "By the way," he added, "I suppose I'd better introduce myself, I'm Billy."

"Yes I know," the gingerbread man said casually.

"How do you know?" Billy puzzled.

"Because I'm magic, and a gingerbread man."

"Oh, I see." Billy said. "So what's your name then?"

"Geronimo," the gingerbread man said.

"But that's an Indian name, isn't it?"

"I don't know," the gingerbread man said. "But I do know it's my name, anyway, because you're now the band conductor, you should go to the front and march us up the hill."

"Oh!" Billy felt a pang of self importance. "Right then," he walked round to the front. "All ready? By the right quick march!" Billy had no idea what by the right meant, but he had seen soldiers say it in films. Anyway, it sounded good to him.

They set off at a cracking pace, Billy proudly at the head of his twenty-four bandsmen, across the floor of the Valley, and up the hill on the far side. He could hear the thud of marching feet behind him; he smiled to himself feeling a bit smug. As the hill got steeper, the pace got slower, and slower, until finally they reached the top of the hill.

"Phew! I'm glad that's over," Billy gasped.

"Hello, you've come back then." The voice seemed familiar. Billy spun round. There sitting leaning back against a tree, with his legs crossed and chewing a rather large carrot, was Dumpy.

"Hello Dumpy," Billy was pleased to see his friend. "Yes I've come back, and these are some new friends of mine. They're musicians you know, and we've come this morning to collect all the instruments for tonight's Ball.

"Really! Well don't make too much noise, will you, I'll be having

a nap shortly." The rabbit finished his carrot, and then snuggled down to sleep. "See you at the Ball." Dumpy lifted one eyelid as he spoke, then he started to snore.

It was the middle of the afternoon, and at a clearing deep in the forest, Billy and the bandsmen were putting the finishing touches to the stage. The drums were set up at the back, and in front of those were the trumpets, trombones and saxophones, then at the front were six violins.

"There!" Billy said happily, "we're almost ready. Just the glow worms for lighting, and that's it." Geronimo cast his experienced eye across the set.

"Hmmm! something's missing," he said, scratching his head thoughtfully. His eyes scanned the scene again and again. "But what?" He paced up and down deep in thought.

"I know!" He said at last, "it's the piano, where is the piano?" Everybody looked at everybody else, as if expecting an answer; but no one had the answer. "Has anybody seen the piano?" he pleaded. But no one had.

After a while, the murmuring of the gingerbread men talking amongst themselves subsided until there was silence. Billy looked around. Most of the gingerbread men were sitting down on the grass, their elbows on their knees, their heads resting in their hands. One or two leaned against trees. The only sound now was the wind rustling the leaves high in the tree tops. Billy seated himself in a similar manner to the gingerbread men. No one spoke. Although Billy had never actually heard the band play, he could well imagine how it would sound without a piano. But where was it? How can you possibly loose a piano?

Billy thought he felt the ground tremble, but he wasn't sure. Then he heard a squeak. Probably a mouse or something he thought. But there it was again, the ground trembled and the squeak, they seemed to come together this time. He looked around at the others, he could see the gingerbread men looking at each other, some were pointing to the distance; it seemed they felt and heard it too. But what was it? Then it came again and again, getting louder and louder. Then one or two of the

gingerbread men started to walk slowly in the direction of the approaching squeak, the ground was shaking even more now. Then curiosity got the better of Billy. He got to his feet and joined the gingerbread men walking in the direction of the squeak. Then they could hear more clearly, the shake and the squeak came almost together, and then came a gasp. Shake, squeak and gasp. They started to trot towards the sound, and then ran, dodging the trees and bushes as they went. Then as they broke into a clearing, they stopped dead in their tracks not believing what they saw. There coming towards them very slowly but surely was a grand-piano, and pushing hard at the single wheel at the narrow point was Mole.

"Mole!" Billy shouted. "What are you doing?"

"I found it in the middle of the trees," Mole panted. "I knew you would need it, so I thought I'd better bring it."

"Oh Mole," Billy said. "You should have come to us for help, not pushed it on your own," Billy chuckled. "Come on lads, lend a hand here."The twenty-four gingerbread men gathered around the Piano and lifted it bodily into the air, carrying it effortlessly to the bandstand.

***

Late afternoon turned to dusk, heralding the arrival of the glow-worms. They took their places in the archway of bushes over the bandstand. Then as dusk turned to darkness they all lit their tails, like stars twinkling in the heavens, and throwing a greeny white light across the dancing area.

Then, in ones and twos, the dancers started to arrive. Rabbits, hedgehogs badgers, foxes and deer, the Snogs came as well. Owls, crows and starlings lined the branches of the trees bordering the clearing, and then the music started. First the piano, then the bass player picked up the tempo, a short while later, the drummer joined in, and then the whole band played boogie woogie and rock and roll. Dumpy was right in the middle of everyone shaking the ground with every step. Billy was at the front of the band waving a stick at the band, he had no idea what he was doing, but nevertheless he was enjoying himself. Out of the corner of his eye he could see Horace boogie-woogie-ing

along the branches of a nearby tree.

The music went on and on, hour after hour, but Dumpy had long since given up, and was puffing and panting against a nearby tree. Then across the dance floor, bouncing on their tails, which were coiled up like springs, came the Snogs. The band played one lively tune after another, after an hour, Billy decided it was time for the band to have a break.

"Right ladies and gentlemen!" He said in his poshest voice. "The next dance will be the Conga, after which there will be a short intermission. Now you all know how to do the Conga, so, when the music starts, all into line and a nice long dance all around the woods."

The band started off in a Latin American rhythm, with Dumpy leading them out of the clearing and into the trees. Billy lost sight of them as they vanished into the darkness. Then suddenly, the band stopped playing. Billy looked up from the music to the musicians. They were all staring past him and into the clearing. Billy spun around to see a man standing in the middle, panting as though he had been running.

"Hello!" Billy said in surprise. "Who are you?"

"I'm so sorry to have startled you," the man said. "But I heard your music, and I've been following the sound to try to find you."

"Oh...I see," Billy said a bit sheepishly. "Has the music been annoying you then?"

"Oh no! Nothing like that." The man said. "But then perhaps I had better introduce myself, I am William Barrett-Forbes," he lifted his arm to shake hands with Billy.

"Are you now," Billy said as he took the man's hand. "So what brings you here then Mr Barrett-Forbes?"

"Well," the man continued. "I am the organiser of the annual carnival in town, which takes place tomorrow."

"So?" Billy wondered what it had to do with him.

"So the band we had booked for the carnival has let us down, and I wondered if perhaps you might play for us instead?"

"Hmmm! I'd better ask.."

"Of course we will." Said twenty-four voices in unison.

"Well that seems to have answered your question, doesn't it." Billy observed.

"There's just one thing," Barrett-Forbes said.

"Which is?" Billy raised his eyebrows.

"You will need some sort of a float. You know a carriage on which you can all ride together. You know what I mean?"

"I know exactly what you mean," Billy said. "I have an idea, and I think we will give you a very big surprise. What time does it start?"

"Two o'clock sharp," said Barrett-Forbes.

"We'll be there!" Billy said excitedly.

***

Billy and the bandsmen worked solidly all night long,with all the animals of the forest helping as much as they could. Gradually, Billy's idea started to take shape. By dawn the float was almost ready.

"One thing puzzles me," Geronimo said scratching his head. "How are we going to move it?"

"Ah ha, I've already thought of that," Billy said. "As soon as it's light, I'll go with Horace to see some friends. But for now, let's all go round to Dumpy's house for a cup of tea. They squashed in to Dumpy's house as best they could, those who couldn't get in, stayed outside, with the tea being passed out to them. And then dawn came, it was time for Billy to shrink down to size, and go with Horace.

***

By a quarter to two everything was ready. All the floats were lined up ready to go, Billy and the gingerbread men were the last following all the other floats into the arena. At two o'clock they could hear all the people in the arena cheering as the first of the procession moved off. Slowly but surely they moved forwards behind the others, until it was time for them to be seen by the people in the arena. Billy deliberately held back creating a gap behind the float in front. "Right boys, are we ready? Let's go!" He waved his baton in the air, and the band started playing. As the float came into view of the people for the first time, a big gasp came from the audience, followed by cheering.

First into view came six pink flamingos, each holding a long pink ribbon in their beaks, which trailed back to six pure white ponies. The float they were pulling had carriage wheels, over the top of which was mounted a fairy castle with the band scattered over it in various places. Then above, flying in a slow circle, were six more pink flamingos. The crowd clapped louder and louder, as the float moved along. Then at the halfway point, six of the musicians exchanged their instruments for violins, and the music changed into waltz time. As the music changed, the six flamingos let go of the ribbons they were holding, and took to the air. Then all twelve flamingos wheeled and swooped in time with the music. Then came all the birds from the woodlands, owls, blackbirds, starlings, wood pigeons and doves, all wheeling and swooping in time with the music.

"Superb, amazing." One man shouted, as he stood up clapping. "Unbelievable!" shouted another, and "I've never seen anything like it," shouted another. Then one by one to start with, then the whole crowd stood cheering and waving, and taking photographs. The local radio reporter rushed up as close as he could get with the microphone, as did the television reporter with his camera, while Billy stood proudly on the front of the float waving his baton, the crowd shouting Bravo! Bravo! Bravo! Echoing in his ears.

***

"You've let your breakfast get cold again Billy!" His mother lifted his plate. "I'll warm it up for you."

"Thank you mother." Billy rubbed his eyes and looked down at the table. There on the two baking trays in front of him, were the twenty-four gingerbread men, twelve on each. Billy wasn't sure, but he thought he saw the gingerbread man nearest him, lift his head and wink.

"There you are Billy; now finish it before it gets cold again. When you've eaten it all, you can have a gingerbread man if you like."

"No, not just now mother, if you don't mind." Billy said, secretly vowing never to eat another gingerbread man, ever. His mother shrugged her shoulders and carried on with her work.

THE ADVENTURES OF BILLY THE BEAN
AVAILABLE NOW...
THE ADVENTURES OF BILLY THE BEAN
BILLY AND THE SNOGS
MAYFAIR
TAXI

THE ADVENTURES OF
BILLY THE BEAN

AVAILABLE NOW...

THE ADVENTURES OF
BILLY THE BEAN

BILLY AND THE DRAGONS OF DUNLAGIN

THE ADVENTURES OF BILLY THE BEAN

AVAILABLE NOW...

THE ADVENTURES OF BILLY THE BEAN
INTRODUCING BILLY THE BEAN

THE ADVENTURES OF
BILLY THE BEAN
COMING SOON...
BILLY THE BEAN AND THE ANCIENT MARINER
ALSO AVAILABLE SOON...
BILLY THE BEAN AND THE HAUNTED FOREST

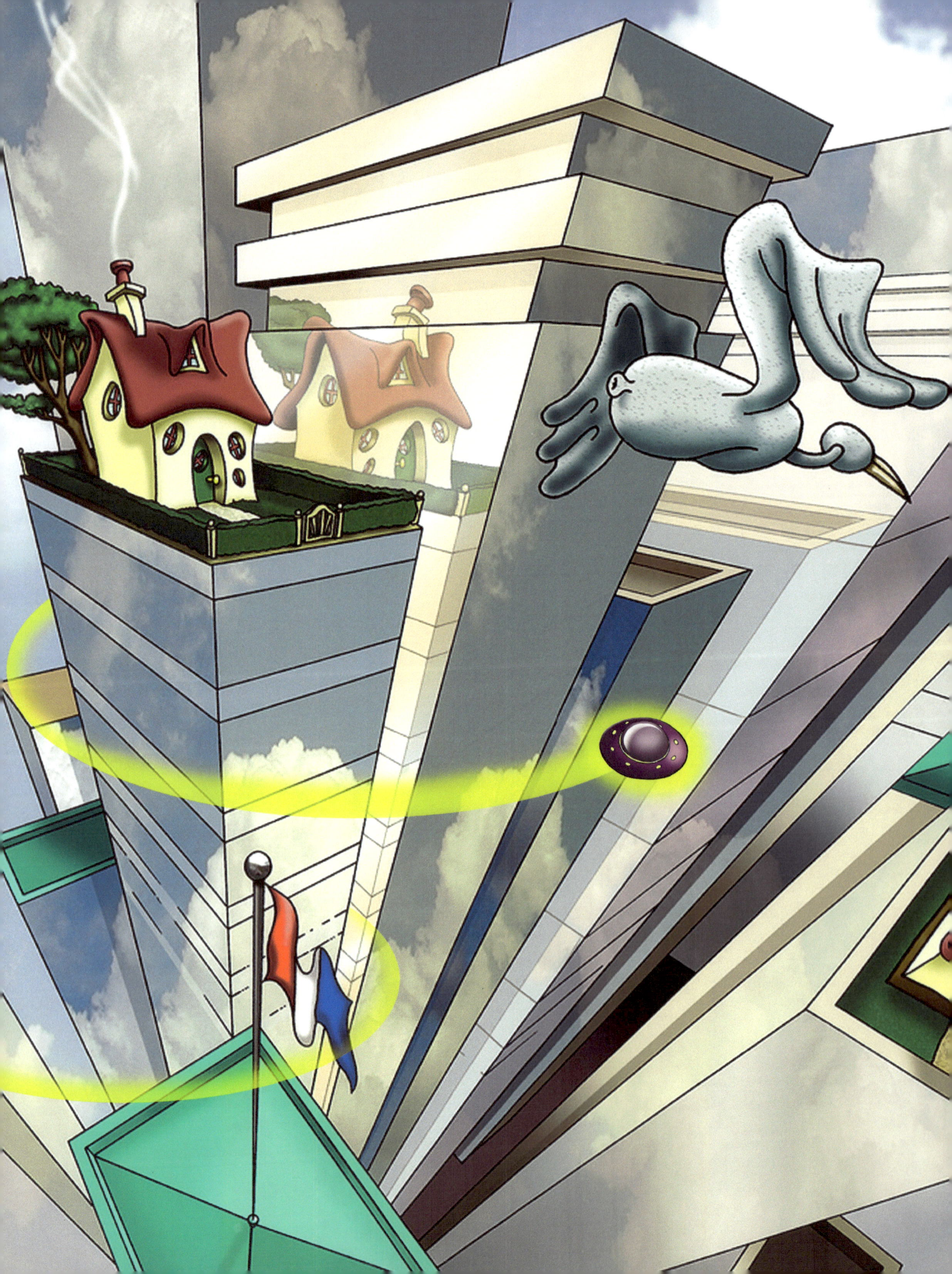

www.ingramcontent.com/pod-product-compliance
Lightning Source LLC
Chambersburg PA
CBHW040848070726
47599CB00029B/612